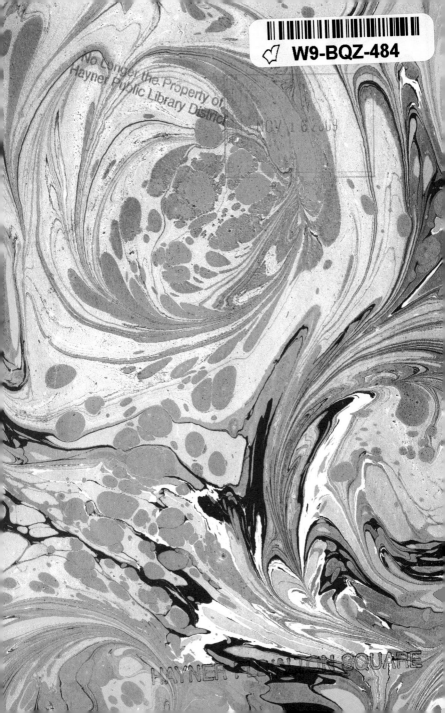

MATCHLESS

Also by Gregory Maguire

FICTION

BOOKS IN THE WICKED YEARS
Wicked
Son of a Witch
A Lion Among Men

Confessions of an Ugly Stepsister
Lost
Mirror Mirror

NONFICTION

Making Mischief: A Maurice Sendak Appreciation

MATCHLESS

—A Christmas Story—

An Illumination of Hans Christian Andersen's Classic
"The Little Match Girl"

WRITTEN AND ILLUSTRATED BY

GREGORY MAGUIRE

WILLIAM MORROW
An Imprint of HarperCollinsPublishers

HarperCollins books may be purchased for educational, business, or
sales promotional use. For information please write: Special Markets
Department, HarperCollins Publishers, 10 East 53rd Street, New York,
NY 10022.

FIRST EDITION

Designed by Kris Tobiassen

Library of Congress Cataloging-in-Publication Data
Maguire, Gregory.
 Matchless: a Christmas story / by Gregory Maguire.—1st ed.
  p. cm.
 Summary: Entwines the classic fairy tale of the little match girl with
a story of Frederik, whose mother is seamstress to the Queen and who
spends many evenings crafting a village in the attic of their small, cold
home.
 ISBN 978-0-06-191301-3
 [1. Fairy tales.] 1. Andersen, H.C. (Hans Christian), 1805–1875. Lille
pige med svovlstikkerne. II. Title.
 PZ8.M2825Mat 2009
 [Fic]—dc22

2009015954

09 10 11 12 13   ID/SCP 10 9 8 7 6 5 4 3 2 1

TO GERALDINE FEGAN

and to the thousands
of school and public librarians
who work to keep
the library lamps burning
during dark times

PART
ONE

ON AN ISLAND so far north that it snowed from September to April, a boy named Frederik kept himself warm by keeping a secret.

SOME MORNINGS the top of the water in the kitchen jug had frozen into a disc of ice. Frederik had to smash it with a wooden spoon.

He piled the pieces of ice in a saucer, reminded of the way that harbor ice broke up in a thaw. Small ice made musical clinking sounds; large ice groaned like his mother.

"Not dawn, not yet!" she protested through her morning congestion. "The troubles of another day come to haunt me. Where are you, my sweet ginger biscuit?"

"I'm making your tea to warm you up," replied Frederik.

HE HURRIED to light the kitchen fire. Money was scarce, and this was the last match until his mother could afford to buy more, so he struck it carefully. The warmth on his fingers made him want—quick—to use them to make something clever before they became stiff with cold again. His fingers were the only clever part of him.

"My useful child," said the widow Pedersen. "Tea on a cold morning: a reason to live. But this"—she grimaced—"pfaah! It's thin as rainwater. Have you made one scoop of leaves do for a whole pot?"

"The canister is nearly empty."

"It's Christmas Eve: I'm paid today. I'll buy some more."

"We need matches, too."

AS DAME PEDERSEN and Frederik folded the bedding, their breath wisped in the chilly room. "Look, it's a pair of ghosts."

"That's all that'll be left of us, a pair of ghosts, unless you succeed today," said Dame Pedersen. "Make those seagulls pay for waking me with their jeering."

"We work as a team, the gulls and I," Frederik reminded her. His stomach muttering with hunger, Frederik kissed his mother and left.

The Pedersens lived in a couple of rooms tacked onto a herring smokehouse on an island in the harbor. From their threshold Frederik looked across the water to the prosperous city on the mainland. The town was bedecked with necklaces of evergreen. Setting out across the low stone causeway that joined island to mainland, Frederik caught a whiff of a goose roasting for a holiday luncheon.

USUALLY HE STAYED near the docks, meeting the boats. As fishermen emptied their nets of herring or skrat or mackerel, gulls or storks filched from the day's catch.

If Frederik could startle a scavenger into dropping a fish, why, there was the beginning of supper. The fishermen didn't begrudge Frederik stealing from seagulls.

WHEN FISH WERE FEW, Frederik searched for bits of beautiful trash. Anything he might use for his secret.

HIS MOTHER didn't suspect a thing. Every night when she came home from the palace—she was a seamstress for the Queen—Dame Pedersen fried the fish and then plunged under the warm coverlet to do her mending there. The Queen had a heavy foot and always stepped on her own hems, so every evening Frederik's mother reached for her basket of threads, all wrapped tightly on wooden spools.

'EVEN ON CHRISTMAS 'EVE she plied her needle. Humming sentimental melodies of the season, she stitched while Frederik washed up. As soon as she nodded off over her scissors, Frederik scampered up the ladder to his attic.

T H E   R O O M reeked with the salt tang of the sea and the sweet rawness of the smokehouse. He didn't mind; this was *his* room, to which his mother in her exhaustion could never manage to climb.

HERE he was not fish-thief, but governor.

ON THE PLANKS of the attic floor waited Frederik's secret: a town hunched on an island, a heap of netting that had washed into his path once when north winds drove the waves clear across the causeway.

The houses were made of empty boxes that he'd lifted from merchants' rubbish bins. Frederik cut out windows and folded the cardboard: perfect hinged shutters. He built eaves out of slates that the wind had liberated from real roofs. He planted trees by poking sprigs of balsam into dollops of boat caulking. Best was the customhouse: a gold-papered chocolate gift box sporting a porcelain dome—an upturned bowl of chipped blue china.

FREDERIK'S TOWN boasted only two residents—two threadless wooden spools with heads made out of acorns. The citizens seemed eager to invite other people to their town, but Frederik didn't know where to find any. Until its thread was used up, Dame Pedersen wouldn't relinquish a spool to serve as company.

FREDERIK HAD DECIDED that the residents should go sailing to hunt for more family. So he was building a harbor out of pebbles. Next he would need a boat.

When someone pounded at the door, his mother started from her nap—"Merciful angels! Have the seagulls grown fists?" Frederik reached the door first.

THE VISITOR SAID to Dame Pedersen, "Our Queen has ripped her cloak on her way to the Christmas Eve ceremonies. She's to preside over prayers and feast and frolic of all varieties; so she demands you come with your supplies! She has sent her coach so I might hurry you along, but dress snug. Ice is even forming on the harbor."

"You would think the Queen has toes of lead," said Dame Pedersen. "She can't see a hem without stepping on it. Still, the hungry rarely get a holiday, so I will come."

"YOU'RE A GOOD WOMAN, to venture out in this cursed cold. Myself, I've had enough of the Queen's misadventures. On Christmas Eve I'd rather be home with my wife or my grog, or both. I intend to seek other employment in the new year."

But Dame Pedersen turned to Frederik. "Dear boy, I've never left you at night before. Will you be safe?"

Frederik nodded.

DAME PEDERSEN bustled away, muttering to the coachman: "One of God's simples, that boy; can't find his way from soap to water. I hate to leave him alone on Christmas Eve."

FREDERIK WAITED until the sound of hooves had faded, and then he wrapped himself in a scarf. His townspeople needed to sail to lonely souls and invite them to live on the island. So Frederik would locate a boat.

PART TWO

IN A LANE off the main square a small girl

shivered in her threadbare shawl.

A L L D A Y she had been hoping to sell the matches in her apron pocket. All day long she had sung: "Light your tapers on Christmas Eve with a new match!" But she hadn't sold a single match, and by nighttime her voice had shriveled. "Matches, I have matches for sale."

SHE DIDN'T DARE go home without a single coin. And home held no warmth, anyway, not since the death of her mother.

She wandered this way and that—how crowded the streets were this late on Christmas Eve!

AS SHE WAS CROSSING the boulevard, a pair of horses dragging a coach raced by. The girl dashed out of their way. The slippers that had belonged to her mother—they were too loose, but they were all the girl had left of her—fell off. A carter's donkey claimed one slipper for its supper. "Oh," cried the match girl, "oh!"

The other slipper might keep *one* foot warm, she thought, but as she went to retrieve it, a boy about her age was picking it up. "This will make a fine cradle for my babies!" he said, and ran off into the darkness so quickly that he never heard her voice calling after him.

THE CROWDS thinned and disappeared. Alone, the match girl tucked herself into an alley, out of the wind but not the cold.

She couldn't go home. And she couldn't sell any matches. So what was there left to do but strike one, to relish the light?

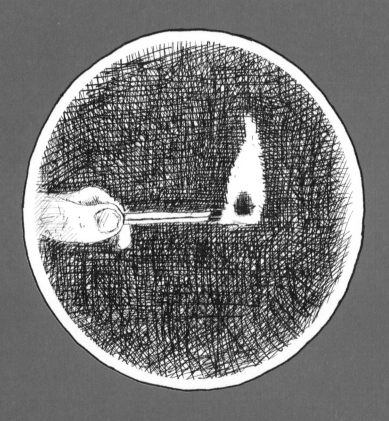

S H E L I T I T—warmth for the tip of her nose, at least—and the tiny blaze confused her eyes. She thought she saw a corner stove with brass trimmings, the door open so the heat could escape. She reached for it—and the match went out.

SHE CROUCHED, half asleep, till a church bell rang. It was a quarter to midnight. So she lit another match, and in the flare she saw a roast goose on a platter, amid silverware and crystal and creamy napery.

"Oh, goose," she called, and it rose on its roasted legs and walked across the table toward her, the knife and fork in its back wagging in a comical way. She laughed, and put her hand to her mouth, but the match burned out and the goose disappeared, and the pretty table with it.

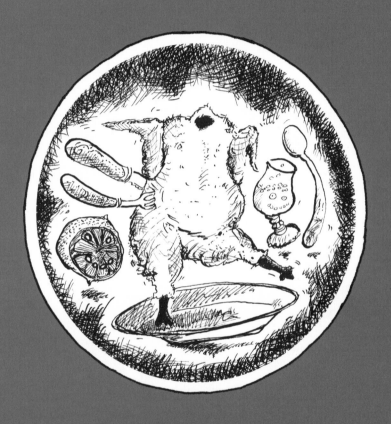

"COME BACK!" She struck a third match.

This time a Christmas tree rose high above her. She craned her head to see the pine boughs laden with glass ornaments, and with candles shining bright as stars. The highest candle served as the beacon; but then it streaked earthward.

"Mother said when a star falls, it means a soul is going up to God; so someone is dying," she remembered.

THEN MIDNIGHT CHIMED, and the thought of her mother cheered her so that the little girl struck another match.

IN THE FLINTY LIGHT she *saw* her mother, who lived in heaven, but who now leaned forward with her smile, her bright and matchless eyes.

AS THE VISION FADED, the match girl despaired, and she lit match after match, to hold the vision. Her mother looked so inviting . . .

. . . AND THEN her warm arms were around the girl; and her mother took her home to the sky, where the stars shine like matches that can never be extinguished.

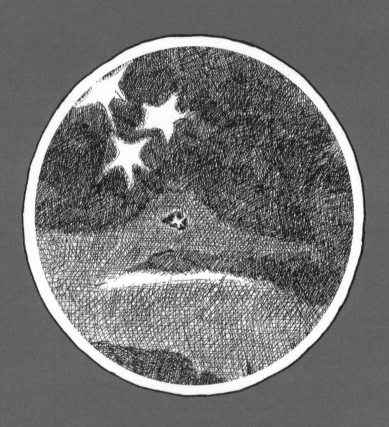

PART
THREE

FREDERIK GOT HOME in time to stir the fire before the coals went out, which was lucky, for he had no way to start a new fire. When his mother returned, she said, "I'd have stopped to buy matches with the Queen's bonus, but I saw no vendors at work this late on Christmas Eve. Now off to your attic; I'll stay by the stove and keep the fire alive till Christmas morn." But sitting to take off her shoes, she leaned against a pillow and immediately fell asleep.

A L L   N I G H T Frederik sat nodding by the stove. Sometimes he imagined climbing into a comfortable shoe and sailing off to find a more hospitable place to live; a place where the poor did not shiver so, and the hungry could find enough to eat, and the children had all the parents they needed. Whenever a coal tumbled, startling him, he tended the fire with a poker, managing to keep the room tolerably warm until dawn.

"CHRISTMAS DAY, my dimpled dumpling!" Oh, la!—precious oranges, and anise cookies, and the fragrant dust of nutmeg to stir into his morning milk.

WHILE DAME PEDERSEN dawdled over her tea, Frederik hurried upstairs to arrange his little folk in their new boat, and help them set sail to find their necessary neighbors and kin. Putting the slipper down, however, he shook something in it loose.

A N I R O N K E Y with a paper tag attached.

Now Frederik guessed that the shoe had been lost by accident. Since he couldn't understand his letters, he plunged downstairs to ask his mother to read the tag. It was an address. "An invitation?" wondered Frederik. "A nuisance," said his mother, but he pestered her until she was overcome. She knew he couldn't find an address on his own, so they made their way hand in hand across the causeway and through quiet streets to locate the address attached to the key.

WHEN YOU'VE NEVER heard its like before, it is hard to recognize the sound of human grief. At first Frederik thought it was seagulls, but his mother insisted: "We have come at an unfortunate moment."

Frederik darted ahead anyway. He pressed through a crowd of neighbors, and he climbed a steep staircase to a room over a warehouse. There he found a frozen girl lying on a table, and her father fitfully rocking nearby, his eyes shut.

"WHO ARE *YOU?* " asked a busybody neighbor. "What business have you, coming here in his time of sorrow?"

"Last night I found this in a lost slipper." Frederik held up the key.

The gossipy neighbor wondered aloud: Was *this* why the girl had not returned? Had she lost her key? And her father, living so high above the warehouse, would never have heard her knocking. He had been out of his mind with work and worry, tending his two babies, who squalled with the consumption that had already claimed his wife and now, it seemed, had stolen his daughter, too.

When Dame Pedersen arrived, puffing from the effort, she covered Frederik's face with her apron while grim-eyed men carried the girl's body away for a pauper's burial.

FREDERIK'S MOTHER motioned that it was time to leave, but then she caught sight of one of the sick babies, grey as bad bacon in the morning light. She had the poor thing to her bosom before she knew what she was doing, so Frederik cradled the other one as best he could. As they held the children, their own family began to change, though they didn't see it at the moment.

WHEN THE YEAR was scarcely a week old, Dame Pedersen helped the match girl's father secure a position as the new coachman to the Queen. And before the year was halfway old, Dame Pedersen had married the man, and invited him and his two frail daughters to share the rooms behind the smokehouse.

T H E FA M I LY WA S still hard-pressed for money, and dreamed of savory treats to eat, but they had the warmth of one another, and enough on which to live, and in most parts of the world that is called plenty.

PART
FOUR

AS THE YEAR surged on, the Queen continued stamping on her hems. There were gowns to be mended every night.

THE FOLLOWING Christmas Eve Frederik's mother decided to spend the night at the palace, leaving her new husband to keep the stove fire burning. She brought her needles and threads, but distracted by kissing her three children, she forgot to take her supper. Frederik offered to carry the meal to his mother. "I *can* find my way," he promised his stepfather.

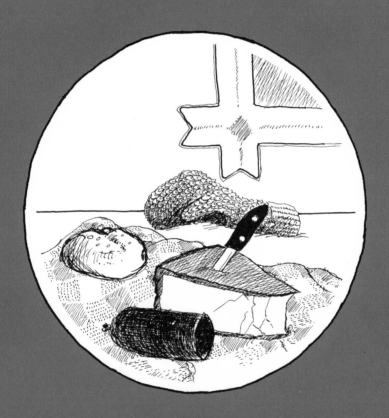

HIS DELIGHTED MOTHER applauded his success at finding the palace, and in holiday spirits, the Queen lunged to hand three pieces of marzipan to Frederik, ripping a royal seam as she did.

HURRYING HOME that Christmas Eve, however, Frederik grew uncertain. An unseasonal thaw was wreathing the city in a clammy mist, disguising the landmarks on which Frederik relied. Tonight it seemed as if all the ghosts of all who had died since last year had risen one last time to see in the holy day.

FREDERIK WASN'T frightened of ghosts, and though the world was masked with vapor, eventually he found the causeway.

Starting across, he heard a belligerent sound. He recognized it as plates of ice jamming in the mouth of the harbor channel, grinding their cold edges against one another. With the outlet plugged, and the snow melting, the harbor was rising. Inches of seawater flooded the causeway.

HE STOOD STILL. He couldn't see his way forward along the causeway, nor could he retrace his steps. A false step would drown him, and no boat in the shape of a mother's slipper would come sidling up to rescue him.

"Oh," he prayed aloud, "let me get home to my sisters! I have marzipan fruits for them!"

T H E   W A T E R lapped higher as bells began to ring in the muffling fog. He blinked, and then he saw a little light, a momentary flare held out by an invisible hand. He reached toward it, and the light went out.

ʙᴜᴛ, ʟᴏᴏᴋ, another!—several feet beyond,

so he took a step forward.

A   THIRD   FLAME winked beyond that . . .

and then a fourth.

SMALL BRIEF LIGHTS, but helpful as matches struck just in time. Frederik followed the chain of evanescent stars across the dark water to safety.

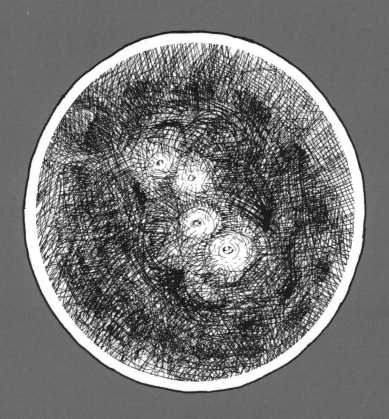

SOME PEOPLE know better than to announce if a little light has appeared to them. Frederik didn't confide in his mother when she returned the next morning, with pastries and lingonberry jam. He wanted to tell his stepfather there were reasons not to be sad on this Christmas anniversary. But he didn't know how.

INSTEAD, he said to his sisters, "Eat up your marzipan. I have a surprise upstairs to show you."

THEN HE CARRIED both girls up the ladder, to share with them his secret town, whose population had enjoyed a marked increase over the past year. His sisters clapped their hands . . .

—OH, how his sisters clapped their hands!—

. . . UNAWARE THAT high above them,

even in the daylight, exists a population of stars.

THE END

A NOTE ON *MATCHLESS*

and Its Inspiration,
"The Little Match Girl,"
by Hans Christian Andersen

Already a success in 1843, Danish writer Hans Christian Andersen wrote "The Little Match Girl" ("Den lille pige med svovlstikkerne") at the invitation of an editor who supplied a selection of illustrations for inspiration. One of the pictures showed a child on the street selling matches—sulfur sticks, *svovlstikkerne*.

Part 2 of *Matchless* follows Andersen's telling almost precisely, although in the interest of drama I have moved the story from New Year's Eve to Christmas Eve. Also, I have allowed the match girl to envision being reunited with her dead mother rather than, as in Andersen, her beloved grandmother.

Unlike the rest of Andersen's most popular tales, "The Little Match Girl" relies on neither magical creatures nor anthropomorphism to work its spell. True, the sacred magic of God's mercy to the poor and dying may obtain in the story's final scene, though readers might as easily interpret the little girl's visions as the delusions of a child freezing to death.

Andersen included the story in his second collection of fairy tales. While "The Little Mermaid," "The Ugly Duckling," and "The Steadfast Tin Soldier" retain their power to charm, the little match girl's plight has come to seem too bleak for modern audiences. In selecting this tale for revisiting—reillumination, perhaps—I hope to honor the original by finding a way to return to the story a sense of the transcendent apprehended by many nineteenth-century readers, children and adults alike.

Matchless was originally written to be heard. It premiered on Christmas Day, 2008, on National Public Radio's *All Things Considered,* in a performance by the author.

Acknowledgments are paid to Cassie Jones, Andy Newman, Jeremy Nussbaum, William Reiss, a nonpareil team of brilliants if ever there was one; to Susan Valdina and Ashley Bryan, who supplied some fishing net for me to draw; and to Ellen Silva of National Public Radio, who extended me an invitation to create a new story for the holidays.

—GREGORY MAGUIRE
April 2009

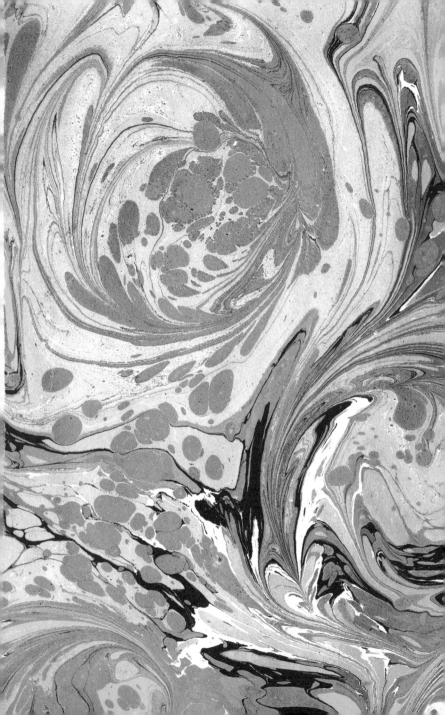